What Do I Look Like?

Nick Sharratt

WALKER BOOKS
AND SUBSIDIARIES

LONDON • BOSTON • SYDNEY • AUCKLAND

What do you look like?

I look like this.

When I'm having fun

I look like this.

When I'm a
scary monster

I look like this.

When I bang
my thumb

I look
like this.

When Cat is a nuisance

I look like this.

When Daddy gives
me ice-cream

I look like this.

When I'm ready for bed

I look like this.

And when I'm fast asleep

I look like this.